Arctic
Ocean

Asia

Europe

Pacific
Ocean

Africa

Indian
Ocean

Oceania

Southern
Ocean

COMINGS and GOINGS

First published in Greece as Φεύγει Έρχεται
by Kaleidoscope Publications in 2017.

Published in the US by Star Bright Books, Inc.
The name Star Bright Books and the Star Bright Books logo
are registered trademarks of Star Bright Books, Inc.

Please visit: www.starbrightbooks.com. For orders,
email: orders@starbrightbooks.com or call: (617) 354-1300.

Hardcover ISBN: 978-1-59572-920-0
Paperback ISBN: 978-1-59572-921-7
Star Bright Books / MA / 00107210
Printed in China / WKT / 9 8 7 6 5 4 3 2 1

Printed on paper from sustainable forests.

Library of Congress Cataloging-in-Publication Data

Names: Kontoleon, Anna, 1974- author. | Kontoleon, Manos, author. |
    Tikkou, Fotini, illustrator.
Title: Comings and goings / Anna Kontoleon, Manos Kontoleon ; illustrations
    by Fotini Tikkou.
Other titles: Pheugei erchetai. English
Description: Cambridge, Massachusetts : Star Bright Books, [2021] |
    "Originally published in Greece by Kaleidoscope Publications in
    2017"--Copyright page. | Audience: Ages 4-8. | Audience: Grades K-1. |
    Summary: As Alex and his parents prepare for Alex's trip to visit
    family, his extended family eagerly prepare for Alex's arrival.
Identifiers: LCCN 2021005445 | ISBN 9781595729200 (hardcover) | ISBN
    9781595729217 (paperback)
Subjects: CYAC: Family life--Fiction. | Travel--Fiction.
Classification: LCC PZ7.1.K6759 Co 2021 | DDC [E]--dc23
LC record available at https://lccn.loc.gov/2021005445

COMINGS and GOINGS

By
Anna Kontoleon and Manos Kontoleon

Illustrated by
Fotini Tikkou

STAR BRIGHT BOOKS
CAMBRIDGE MASSACHUSETTS

Alex

Alex's mother

Those who went North

Alex's father

Snow the dog

Uncle Mike

Grandpa Leander and Grandma Alexia

Those who stayed South

Aunt Sophie

the twins, Sam and Tina

Plato the parrot

Alex woke up to the ring of his alarm clock. He got up and ran to the calendar. He marked the day with an X. Four more days to go!

Alex dressed and went up to the attic. Among the boxes, he uncovered a small black suitcase covered in dust. *Oh, this won't work*, he thought. Alex slumped back down to his room and got ready for school. It was raining—again!

Grandpa Leander counted the days. "Only four more to go," he muttered, holding a cup of coffee and typing WEATHER FORECAST on his computer. *Will there be any storms in four days?* Leander wondered. None! No wind or rain either.

"Thank goodness for that," he sighed. "We wouldn't want Alex traveling in bad weather." But one never knew with the weather in northern countries . . .

At school, Alex couldn't concentrate or answer the teacher's questions. His mind was elsewhere.

He didn't write in his notebook. He just drew an airplane taking off without him.

After school, Alex and his father visited a department store.

He picked out a red suitcase, a blue bag, and a green backpack.

"Four more days to go," Grandma Alexia said as she made the bed.

She chose the white sheets with the blue wave pattern for Alex's visit. He will sleep in the same room as his mother did when she was a girl!

On the table, she left a picture she had found, of a young girl holding a cat. Alexia smiled. In four days she would be putting to sleep a little boy who now lived far away. And she would tell him stories about his mom when she was a little girl.

When Alex and his father got home, Alex opened his toy box and took out his two favorite cars. From his bookshelf, he picked out the three books in the *Adventures of Tiger Leo* series. Alex then packed his chess set and a few table games. He squeezed everything into his new backpack.

Aunt Sophie went to a bookshop.

"I am looking for a present for a six-year-old boy. He lives far away and I would like a book to show him our city."

The assistant suggested a book full of maps and pictures.

Sophia was thrilled. "This is perfect," she said. One day soon, she would take Alex and the twins on a walk around the city to uncover its secrets.

The next morning, Alex woke up before his alarm clock rang. He marked another X on the calendar. Three more days to go!

Alex dressed warmly and got ready for school. After school, Alex's mom met him. She wanted to take Alex to a quaint shop in the city's old neighborhood.

"I bought Alex this bicycle!" Uncle Mike exclaimed to Leander, his father.

Leander looked at the red bike. "Why doesn't it have training wheels?"

"I want to be the one to teach Alex how to ride a bicycle so he will always remember me," said Mike.

"Are you sure it's safe?" Leander asked. "Why don't you teach him how to tie his shoelaces? That way he will think of you every morning for the rest of his life!"

Alex enjoyed doing a lot of things with his mother, but shopping was not one of them. He got dizzy and felt like running away.

With great effort, he managed to choose:

A printed shawl for Grandma Alexia.

A hat with a feather for Grandpa Leander.

A big beer glass for Uncle Mike.

A bag of herbs for Aunt Sophie.

A box of milk chocolates for the twins.

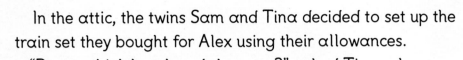

In the attic, the twins Sam and Tina decided to set up the train set they bought for Alex using their allowances.

"Do you think he already has one?" asked Tina, who was afraid Alex wouldn't appreciate their gift.

"He might," said Sam as he added the last part of a bridge, "but it is one thing to play alone. It is another to play together."

Tina sighed, hoping her brother was right.

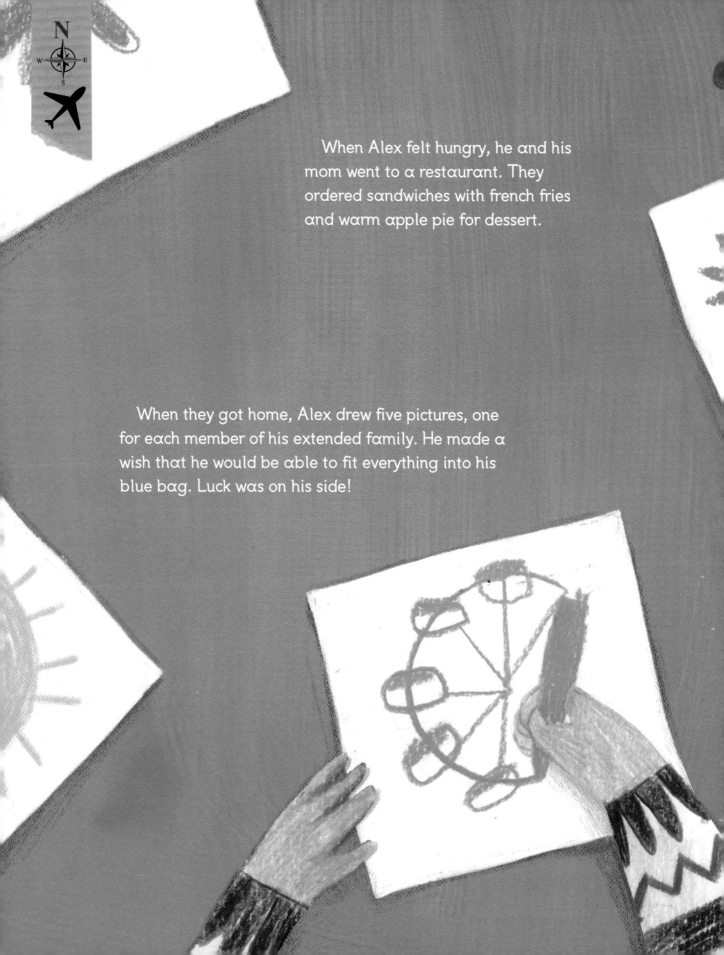

When Alex felt hungry, he and his mom went to a restaurant. They ordered sandwiches with french fries and warm apple pie for dessert.

When they got home, Alex drew five pictures, one for each member of his extended family. He made a wish that he would be able to fit everything into his blue bag. Luck was on his side!

Three more days to go, Leander thought as he walked among the rides in an amusement park.

"Can a six-year-old boy ride in one of these?" he asked the lady selling tickets for the bumper cars.

"Only if you sit next to him," she explained.

Leander thought of the first time he rode in a bumper car with his mother. He must have also been around six.

The next day, Alex woke up before anyone else, just as the warm rays of sun made their first appearance. He marked another X. Two more days to go!

From his wardrobe, he took a pair of blue shorts, green pants, a checkered shirt, his favorite yellow T-shirt, two striped vests, some underwear, and his brown sandals.

Alexia walked to the fruit market with a list of Alex's favorite things. "Now, let's see . . . bananas, apples, apricots . . . What else? . . . Cherries, of course!"

Alexia asked the vendor, "Are the cherries good?"

"Please, taste for yourself!" replied the young seller.

"Mmm, so good!" Alexia said. "I am sure they can't get fruit like this in the north."

Alex's yellow T-shirt had a big stain! Cleaning his shirt made Alex late for his last day of school. He didn't have time for breakfast.

On the way to school, Alex kept bumping into things because he looked up at the sky.

Sophie typed on the computer: **What are the best plays for children?**

Little Red Riding Hood, Peter Pan . . .

"These are probably for younger children . . . Alex is a grown-up boy now," she sighed.

Stories From Our Myths she read, also noting the venue. Sophia was sure this would be a good play for Alex and the twins.

Alex hoped the clouds would stay away. And, to his surprise, they did! The clouds moved toward the mountains.

As soon as he got home, Alex ran to the window. His yellow T-shirt was dry. He shoved it into his red suitcase.

"What's that?" Leander asked Mike.

"It's a skateboard, Dad!" Mike exclaimed.

"Aren't you a bit old for that?"

"I bought it for Alex! I am going to teach him how to balance so he will always remember me," Mike said with a smile.

"Are you sure it is safe?" asked Leander. "Why don't you teach him how to tie his shoelaces? That way he will think of you every morning for the rest of his life!"

The next morning, Alex woke up before the first rays of sun began to shine, just as the neighborhood baker started making his strudel cakes. It was the first day of summer vacation. He marked one more X in his calendar. Only one more day to go!

All his things were packed. The blue bag and green backpack were both full. His red suitcase still had room for a few more things.

"Will it be ready by tomorrow?" asked Tina.
Her brother didn't answer. The twins were building a
tree house to play in with Alex.
"And will it be strong enough for all three of us?"
wondered Tina.

"Do you think we may also have to
leave someday, like Alex?" Tina asked.
She was happy that they lived here, in a
house with a big tree in the garden.

After a hearty breakfast, Alex opened the closet and found the striped summer bag. Good thing it wasn't in the dusty attic!

He took out two bathing suits, a straw hat, a beach towel, a bucket, a spade, and a rake.

Alex also grabbed flippers, goggles, a snorkel, a net, a water pistol, a frisbee, two paddles, and three ping-pong balls.

"Tomorrow is the big day!" exclaimed Leander, carrying many packages.

"What's all this?" asked Alexia.

Leander opened one of the packages. "These are foam bricks to help you float. Do you think they will fit around Alex's waist?"

Alexia smiled.

Leander opened the rest of the packages, full of life vests and inflatable toys in all colors and shapes . . .

Alexia burst out laughing.

Alex carried everything to his room and tried to fit it all in his red suitcase. He squeezed, pushed, and sat on the suitcase. But Alex couldn't close it. He burst into tears.

Alex's mom walked in and helped him sort it all out. "Grandpa Leander and Grandma Alexia will have a beach towel," she said. "And the twins can share their summer toys."

Mike placed five boxes on the table.

"What's all this?" asked Alexia as she unwrapped them.

Each one had a pair of shoes, and they all had shoelaces.

"For Alex," explained Mike.

Leander shook his head. "That's good . . . He is sure to learn how to tie his shoelaces this way. And he will think of you every morning for the rest of his life!"

In the evening, Alex had difficulty going to sleep. He heard the wind and rain against the window. Just as the baker put strudel in the oven, as the sun's rays appeared on the horizon, as the first train of the day left the platform, and as the alarm was ready to go off, he at last fell asleep.

When his mother woke him up, Alex felt exhausted. Dad had already put the luggage in the car.

Sophie rested her coffee on the table. "We will celebrate Alex's arrival today!"
"Are we going to have a party?" asked Sam.
"Not a simple party," Sophie said. "We are going to celebrate at the Dinosaur Theme Park!"

Peter
Constance
Helen
Nicholas
George
Marina

Tina wrote down a list of all the children they would invite. "Alex will never forget this party!"

Imagine celebrating in the company of a Tyrannosaurus rex and Triceratops . . .

The big airplane was waiting, proud and grand, on the tarmac. The flight attendant hung a nametag around Alex's neck. Dad hugged him and Mom kissed him. Alex felt squeezed between the two of them.

A flight attendant took Alex by the hand. Mom and Dad waved through the glass. Alex felt a pinch in his heart.

Alexia rolled out a long piece of paper on the floor. Next to her were two long poles, paint, and paintbrushes. She was in a hurry. All had to be ready before they left for the airport!

She thought of the surprise on Alex's face when he would see what she had prepared. The two of them shared the same name . . .

"You took my name!" Alex said to her when he was two. Alexia had laughed then. And here she was laughing again.

The pilots welcomed Alex and showed him
around the cockpit. The flight attendant took him
to his seat by the window and offered him a piece
of candy. Alex kept his eyes open until takeoff, but
then quickly fell asleep.

When Alex opened his eyes, the plane was
flying over the big, blue sea. A bright sun warmed
his face.

"Come on, everyone. We are going to be late!" cried Sophie.

Sam ran to his room. From his desk drawer he took out a little box of candies. "Are you sure Alex will like them?" he asked his sister.

Tina tucked the box into her backpack.

"Let's go, Sam and Tina," called Sophie. "Grandpa, Grandma, and your father are already on their way!"

The twins ran to get into the backseat.

The airplane landed gently. A flight attendant greeted
Alex with a smile and led him to the baggage claim.
Although the conveyor belt was packed with luggage, Alex
had no trouble spotting his own bags.
    The flight attendant stood with Alex. He took a deep breath.

Alex's family met in the parking lot.

"We are late!" Leander was upset.

They almost ran into the Departures terminal. The big doors opened and closed.

All six of them lined up and looked for Alex. Leander and Mike stood at the far end of the baggage claim, holding the welcome banner.

Alex hesitated and looked around.

Then he saw them . . .

And they saw him . . .

They were all there! Grandpa Leander and Grandma Alexia, Uncle Mike and Aunt Sophie with the twins, Tina and Sam. And a loving banner!

North
America

Pacific
Ocean

South
America

Atlantic
Ocean